KEELEY

THE GIRL FROM
TURTLE MOUNTAIN

DEBORAH ELLIS

KEELEY

THE GIRL FROM TURTLE MOUNTAIN

DEBORAH ELLIS

PENGUIN
CANADA

PENGUIN CANADA

Penguin Group (Canada), a division of Pearson Penguin Canada Inc.,
10 Alcorn Avenue, Toronto, Ontario M4V 3B2

Penguin Group (U.K.), 80 Strand, London WC2R 0RL, England
Penguin Group (U.S.), 375 Hudson Street, New York, New York 10014, U.S.A.
Penguin Group (Australia) Inc., 250 Camberwell Road, Camberwell, Victoria 3124, Australia
Penguin Group (Ireland), 25 St. Stephen's Green, Dublin 2, Ireland
Penguin Books India (P) Ltd, 11, Community Centre, Panchsheel Park, New Delhi – 110 017, India
Penguin Group (New Zealand), cnr Rosedale and Airborne Roads, Albany,
Auckland 1310, New Zealand
Penguin Books (South Africa) (Pty) Ltd, 24 Sturdee Avenue, Rosebank 2196, South Africa

Penguin Group, Registered Offices: 80 Strand, London WC2R 0RL, England

First published 2004

1 2 3 4 5 6 7 8 9 10   (WEB)

NATIONAL LIBRARY OF CANADA CATALOGUING IN PUBLICATION

Ellis, Deborah, 1960–
Keeley : the girl from Turtle Mountain / Deborah Ellis.

(Our Canadian girl)
ISBN 0-14-301484-6

I. Title. II. Series.

PS8559.L5494K44 2003   jC813'.54   C2003-905022-X

Visit the Penguin Group (Canada) website at **www.penguin.ca**

To Kim and Deanna

my two nieces

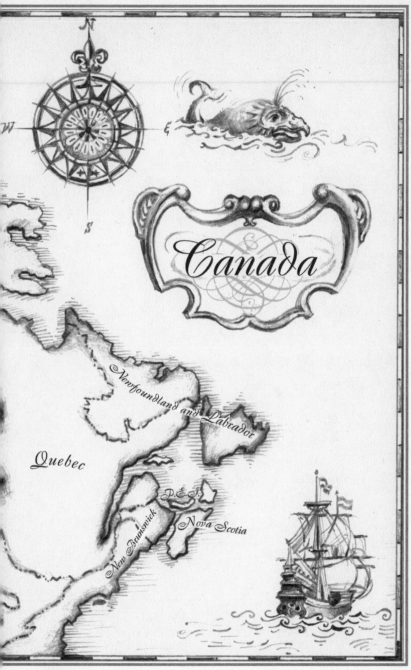

Canada

N
W   E
S

Newfoundland and Labrador

Quebec

P.E.I.

New Brunswick

Nova Scotia

 Marks the location of the story

MEET KEELEY

K EELEY IS JUST TURNING NINE YEARS OLD when we first meet her. Since her mother's death, she has been living with her very strict grandparents while her father has been away getting whatever work he could in the coal mines of the West. But all that is about to change.

Canada's hunger for coal at the start of the twentieth century had mining companies scrambling to find new deposits and build new mines. Keeley and her father are about to move into a brand-new town called Frank, a town created to support a new coal mine deep in the heart of Turtle Mountain, in what is now known as the Crowsnest Pass region of the Rocky Mountains. Frank was a blend of the amenities of town life and of the wildness of the frontier. There was room for people to stretch out and for women, especially, to do things they might be discouraged from doing in larger, more settled places.

The sixty-mile-long Crowsnest Pass area straddles the border between southern British Columbia and Alberta. At the time of this story, the region was part of the vast area called the North-West Territories. *Pass* is a term given for a narrow passage through a mountain range. Frank is in a valley, right at the bottom of Turtle Mountain.

The town has attracted a strange assortment of people, some of whom have settled in, while others are just passing through, hoping, perhaps, to make enough money to be able to go farther north to the Yukon, where gold has recently been discovered.

Keeley arrives in Frank on the day the town is celebrating its first official birthday, and there is excitement all around her about what the future will hold. Not even rumours about Turtle Mountain being "on the move," as the Kootenay Indians say, dampen people's spirits.

For Keeley the best part of living in Frank is that her father can get a job in the mine and they can be together. Living in Frank offers Keeley three things she loves—her father, freedom, and fun.

Will it all turn out the way she hopes? Read on and find out.

CHAPTER N° 1

Keeley stared hard at the strange-looking bird on the hat of the woman in front of them. Every time the train bobbed, the bird bobbed with it.

"Pop, is that bird real?" She tugged at her father's sleeve to make him look.

Keeley and her father were standing in the aisle of the train, squished in with the others who were not lucky enough to get seats. Pop didn't answer her. He was busy listening to the Company man standing at the front of the car, making a speech. The Company man shouted to be heard over the chug-chug of the train.

Keeley began to feel queasy from staring so hard at the bobbing bird. She switched her stare to the precious bundle on the luggage rack above the seats, the one that held her mother's paintings. It was safe, but Keeley still felt wobbly. She closed her eyes and tried to pay attention to the speech.

"You will witness the birth of a brand-new town," the man from the Canadian-American Coal and Coke Company boomed out dramatically. "And for this event, special trains are bringing you from the great cities of Lethbridge and Cranbrook, trains laid on by the Canadian Pacific Railway out of the goodness of their hearts."

"And their desire for coal," a woman behind Keeley said. Keeley tried to find the source of the voice, but the people around her were too tall.

"We encourage you all to enjoy yourselves, to take full advantage of all the pleasures offered at this, the biggest birthday celebration in the history of the Dominion of Canada."

At the word *birthday,* Keeley grinned. September 10 was her birthday, too. Only, she was born in 1892, not 1901. She was nine years old today.

I'm older than a town, she thought. She imagined being the big sister to a whole town. "Eat your vegetables!" she could say to the entire town, and "Stop annoying me!" The whole town would have to obey.

Keeley laughed out loud at that thought. Unfortunately her laugh came at the same moment the Company man paused for a breath. Her laugh was heard by everyone in the carriage.

The woman with the funny-bird hat turned and frowned at Keeley. The woman's sour face did not match her bright hat.

Keeley looked up at her father. Pop was smiling down at her. She smiled back. The sour-faced lady faced the front again. The bird on her hat bobbed and swayed.

The Company man kept talking: "You may be asking, Why are we doing this? Why are we throwing such a big party with free food, free entertainment, and free tours of the mine? The answer is simple. Because we are looking for people to join our happy Frank family."

Keeley already knew that. So did everyone else on the train. Jobs were being offered in the new town of Frank, and Keeley's father was hoping to get one of those jobs.

If he did, it would mean they could move out of Keeley's grandparents' house in Lethbridge, where they'd been living for the past two years since Keeley's mother died. They had been staying in Winnipeg before that. Most of the time, Keeley had lived alone with her grand-parents. Pop was usually away, trying to find work.

"I'll get a job in Frank." Pop was certain. "I'm an experienced coal miner. They'll need men with experience."

He was so certain that he and Keeley had packed up their few belongings and brought everything with them to Frank. It was packed in the rack above the train seats. There wasn't much. What they had before, they'd sold to pay for doctors and medicine for Keeley's mother.

The trip to Frank was Keeley's birthday present. If Pop got a job, they could stay together, and her present would last forever. Her grandparents were nice, but very old, and when they weren't falling asleep in their chairs, they were telling her to be quiet.

"You need not be afraid of uprooting your families," the Company man shouted. "You can plant them here and watch them grow. Turtle Mountain is loaded with coal, coal the Dominion needs to warm its homes, run its factories—"

"And fill your pockets," said the woman behind Keeley.

Keeley spun around. This time she saw who made the comment. Other people were looking at her disapprovingly, too, but the woman didn't seem to mind. She was dressed more plainly than the other carefully groomed women. She wore a black broad-brimmed hat, and a strand of hair hung in her face as though she had been too busy to tie it back properly.

Keeley thought she looked interesting. Most interesting of all was the way she scribbled in a notebook.

Keeley had known other scribblers back in Winnipeg. Mostly, they were poets, like her father, although they also had to do other things besides write poetry. "We can always stretch the soup," her mom would say, laughing, whenever one of the scribbling people showed up at dinnertime. Her mother had painting friends; her father had scribbling friends. They were always kind to her, and they made life interesting.

She hadn't seen any painters or scribblers in Lethbridge. It made her feel good to see the broad-hatted woman scribbling.

Then people moved and blocked Keeley's view.

Keeley was tired of standing. It had been fun for a while, keeping her balance while the train jostled, but now her feet were getting sore, and she was tired of looking at other people's chests and hats. If only she could see out a window.

A short while later, the train began to slow down. They had arrived!

Keeley had to see what the world was like outside the train. She bent down low, trying to see outside the window. She wasn't alone in doing this. Everyone was eager to see the new town.

By standing on one foot and twisting a little to the side, Keeley had a few inches of clear view. It wasn't enough. All she could see were parts of things, but she couldn't tell what they were parts of.

She leaned over a bit more, hovering slightly over the hat with the strange bird. This close, Keeley could tell that the bird was a fake, but that wasn't what interested her at the moment.

The window-greedy woman who was blocking Keeley's view moved slightly to say something to her neighbour. For a brief moment, Keeley had a clear view of the world.

The train lurched. Keeley lurched with it.

The leg she was balancing on slipped, and she fell headfirst over the funny-bird hat and into the sour-faced woman's lap.

For a long, horrible moment, Keeley's legs waved in the air. Her hands grabbed out blindly to find something she could use to steady herself. Her fingers closed around something soft and furry.

"A rat!" she screamed, throwing it as far as she could, given her ridiculous posture.

Shrieks and screams filled the train car, drowning out the Company man. Keeley could feel the crowd in the aisle pushing and shoving around her in a panic to get away from the rat.

Strong hands lifted her off the sour-faced woman's lap and stood her upright among the shoving, shrieking throng. Pop held on to her tightly so she wouldn't get swept away.

"Everybody calm down!" the Company man shouted even louder than the screeching. "There is no rat! Look—no rat!"

He held up the sour-faced woman's funny-bird hat. Attached to it was a clump of hair that Keeley hoped was a wig.

Silence dropped on the train liked a boulder. Then the laughter started as titters, and soon everybody in the train was laughing, except Keeley, her father, the Company man, and the sour-faced woman.

The Company man kept a straight face as he made his way through the train car, carrying the hat with the hair attached to it as if it were King Edward's crown. The crowd scrunched aside to let him through. Bowing slightly, he handed the hat to the woman who owned it. She nodded her thanks.

The train came to a complete stop. The Company man held out his arm, and the sour-faced lady, holding her hairy hat, walked in front of him through the car and out of the train, her back straight and her head high.

The show over, people gathered their belongings and moved to the exit like cattle through a corral gate.

Keeley and her father were among the last to leave the train.

"I sure hope she's not moving to Frank," Keeley said.

Keeley's pop laughed loud and hard, and swooped Keeley up in one of his famous hugs. Then they took down their belongings from the luggage rack. Pop let Keeley carry the bundle of her mother's paintings. She wrapped her arms around it and followed her father out of the train.

CHAPTER N⁰ 2

"*In just a few minutes, the new town of* Frank will be officially born."

Being freed from the train did not mean they were freed from having to listen to speeches. Keeley balanced on one leg then the other, wishing the long line of whiskered men on the platform, all named Sir, would stop talking so she could start enjoying her birthday. On and on and on they talked. If children talked that much, there would never be any time to play.

Keeley was close enough to the front to see one of the important-looking men on the platform squint into the sun as he made his speech. He tilted his hat down lower over his eyes and continued: "But before that historic moment happens, we want to hear from our distinguished guests."

The crowd groaned. They were as impatient to get on with the party as Keeley was.

"Enough talking," a man beside her said. "I didn't vote for this windbag. Why do I have to listen to him?"

"Quiet!" someone else said. "Show some respect. He works with the prime minister."

"That doesn't make him any less boring," the man replied.

"At least you got to vote," a woman's voice said. "You haven't been denied the franchise simply because you're a woman."

Keeley peered around and saw that the voice came from the broad-hatted woman she'd seen on the train.

"Madam, if the good Lord had wanted women to vote, He would have made them men!"

A noisy debate followed, with many people adding their opinions. It helped to pass the time while the politicians were talking.

Finally the speeches ended and the "momentous event" took place. The new town of Frank, in Canada's North-West Territories, was born, but all that happened was that one of the speech-makers cut a ribbon while the others smiled for the camera. Keeley was a little disappointed, but not too much. She was used to grown-ups making a big deal out of unimportant things.

"There's something for everyone today!" The Company man went through the crowd shouting about exciting events to come. "Tour the mine. Tour the town. There will be foot races and a thrilling lacrosse game between the long-standing rivals from Blairmore and Pincher Creek. And, to top it all off, an excellent lunch provided to you by the founders of Frank, which will finish off with one ton of ice cream and one ton of fresh fruit, shipped in all the way from Spokane, Washington!"

The crowd broke up. Keeley and Pop strolled down the wooden sidewalks of Dominion Street, Frank's main street. They'd left their bags at the train station to make walking around easier.

"The town's already built," Keeley said. "I thought today was its birthday."

"That's just something they said to get people excited," Pop said. "Towns rarely have real birthdays. They just happen because people find a place where they'd like to live."

The town already had a street full of shops, two hotels, and a large white house that Pop said was a boarding house.

A row of horse-drawn wagons rolled down the dirt street, filled with people. A sign on the wagons said "Mine Tour."

"Are we going to tour the mine?" Keeley asked.

"No," Pop replied. "I'll soon see enough of it if I get a job there. And mines are not places where children should be."

"But you told me that boys often work in mines."

"Just because it happens, doesn't make it right," was Pop's reply.

Keeley didn't mind. The day was sunny and warm. Turtle Mountain rose over the town as if it were giving Frank a big, protective hug. "The mountain looks like it came from one of Mama's paintings," she said. "Do you think she would have liked it here?"

They stopped walking while Pop looked around him and thought. "Your mother was an artist. She could find beauty anywhere and paint it onto a canvas, making it even more beautiful. Here, with the mountain and the valley, and lots of new faces coming together to take part in a new adventure, she'd find many things to paint. Yes, she would have been very happy."

They were quiet for a moment, each with his or her own memories. Then Pop asked, "What do you think? Would you like to live here?"

Keeley looked back at the little town they had just walked through. Compared with Lethbridge, Frank was awfully rough. But Lethbridge had seemed rough at first, too, compared with Winnipeg. There was room here, room for her to run, room for her to spin around without breaking anything, and room for her to make happy noises without bothering anyone.

"Yes," she said. "I'd like to live here."

"All right, then," Pop said. "Let's go find the big bosses of this place and let them know how lucky they are that you and I have come to town."

CHAPTER № 3

While Pop went off to find the employment office, Keeley was free to wander on her own. That was another thing she loved about being with her father. He believed that children needed room to breathe and that they knew how to act with good sense. Her grandmother believed children were always up to no good and should be watched closely. It was a good thing her grandparents slept so much. That was the only way Keeley got any privacy.

It was fun to stroll around the little town. Everyone around her was in a holiday mood.

17

A crowd was collecting in the meadow behind Dominion Street. Keeley poked her way through the people to see what was going on. When she saw kids gathering at the starting line for a foot race, she joined in.

"Hey—this race is for boys. You can't run!"

"It's my birthday. I can do anything I want."

"But you can't—"

The starting pistol went off in the middle of the boy's sentence. He might have kept talking, but Keeley wasn't around to hear him. She was running.

She ran so fast she didn't notice her hat blow away. The cheers of the crowd felt like a cushion of air. Her feet didn't seem to touch the ground, and she flew across the finish line ahead of all the boys.

"I won! I won!" she yelled, dancing around, too excited to stand still and catch her breath.

"She should be ashamed."

An angry voice reached Keeley's ears through her excitement. She stopped dancing and looked around. She could tell from the expressions on some faces that not everyone was happy for her.

"It's her mother who should be ashamed," Keeley heard. "I'd never allow a daughter of mine to make such a display of herself."

Keeley flung herself at the woman. "My mother loved to watch me run! How dare you say anything bad about my mother!"

The women gasped, clutching themselves in horror at such a display of temper, and backed away.

Keeley yelled after them, "She would be proud of me for winning!"

"I won. You didn't," said the boy who'd been beside her at the finish line. "Besides, you're a mess. Look at her hair," he said to the other boys. "She looks like a witch."

"Did you use your broomstick to win the race?" another boy jeered.

"No, just my own two legs, which are much faster than yours." Keeley knew her hair was a mess. Pop wasn't much good at braiding. During the race, one of the strings holding her plaits together had fallen off. She flung her loose hair in the boy's face. "Now, get out of my way. I have a first-place medal to collect."

She strode off to the platform, where her prize awaited. The boys ran after her.

"She can't win, can she?" They crowded around the judge, demanding an answer. "Peter should win." Peter, the second-place finisher, nodded vigorously.

The judge smiled at Keeley, but Keeley didn't believe the smile. She was right. "This race was for the boys," he said. "You understand."

"But there wasn't a race for girls," Keeley said, but she had to say it to the judge's back. She watched him pick the first-place medal off the table and start to hand it to Peter.

"'Prime Minister's Emissary Snubs Little Girl,'" a woman's voice said. "Should make a good headline."

Keeley, the judge, and the boys looked at the broad-hatted woman who was writing in her notebook. The judge frowned, then snorted, but he put the ribbon with the first-place medal on it around Keeley's neck and even managed to mumble, "Congratulations," before walking away.

The boys made faces at Keeley. "I'll get you," Peter said, but Keeley didn't care. She pushed past him and the other boys and ran after the woman in the broad-brimmed hat.

She touched the woman on the arm, but felt suddenly shy when the woman turned around. "I . . . I just wanted to show you my medal," she said, holding it up.

"Very nice—and well deserved. What is your name?"

"Keeley O'Brien."

"Well, Keeley O'Brien, you just took on the minister of the Interior for the Dominion of Canada. That's the first time I've seen that old sod head change his mind."

"Is he a friend of yours?"

The woman roared with laughter. "He's no friend of mine, and I'm no friend of his. My name is Cora Hind." She shook Keeley's hand firmly. "I'm a reporter. I find out what people are up to, and I write about it."

"A reporter? I thought you were a poet."

The woman laughed again. "Why would you think I'm a poet?"

"All the people I've known who wrote things down were poets."

"I'd like to see my editor's face if I turned in a poem instead of a story." Cora Hind laughed.

"I think it's hard to be a poet. Is it hard to be a reporter?"

"Just keep your eyes open and your ears open, and learn how to put a sentence together so you can tell other people what you see and hear. There are plenty of women reporters, and there will be plenty more." Cora Hind gave Keeley another firm handshake and walked away.

Keeley spied her father in the crowd. He was talking with some other men. "Pop, guess what? I met a newspaper reporter, a woman, and I won the foot race!"

"That's my Keeley," he said. He was pleased but not surprised. He expected her to do great things. That was why Keeley loved him.

CHAPTER N° 4

Keeley was so excited about her own news that for a moment she forgot to ask Pop about his. "Did we get it?" she asked. "Did we get a job?"

Pop grinned a big grin and handed her a letter of employment. "We got a job."

Keeley whooped and danced around, waving the letter. She knew she was making a display of herself again, but so what? It was fun.

Pop put his arm around her, trying to calm her down so that he could talk to her.

"It's the boarding house for us," Pop said. "Probably for a long while. Mining doesn't pay what it should, so don't get your hopes up about moving into one of those little houses you like."

The mining company had built dozens of little houses for miners to live in with their families. Keeley thought they were the loveliest little houses she had ever seen.

"The boarding house will be fine," she said. "It will be perfect, in fact. Let's go there now to make sure they have room for us. If they don't have any room, will we have to turn down the job?"

"If there's no room at the boarding house, we'll sleep in the stable. If there's no room in the stable, we'll sleep with the goats in the shed."

"And if there's no room in the shed, we'll sleep in the henhouse with the chickens," said Keeley, laughing. She swung her pop's hand as they walked down the sidewalk toward the large white boarding house.

Outside the saloon, a small girl stood on an upturned crate, peering into the saloon window.

"What's she looking at?" Keeley asked Pop.

"Only one way to find out."

Keeley dropped Pop's hand and ran over to the girl. "What are you looking at?"

The girl turned around. She had a small narrow face and great big glasses.

"Grown-ups are strange," the girl said. She made room for Keeley on the crate. Keeley stepped up and stood beside her at the window.

The poker tables all had men around them, but they were just sitting, and that wasn't very interesting. "Not them, the men at the bar," the girl said.

Keeley looked. One of the men was waving his boot at another man. They were both yelling and swaying. The bartender slammed his towel down on the bar, came around to the front, grabbed a man in each hand, and shoved them towards the front door. Keeley and the other girl turned in time to see the two men fly out the swinging doors onto the sidewalk. The saloon keeper tossed the men's hats out after them, wiped his hands together, nodded pleasantly to Pop and the two girls, then went back into the saloon.

Keeley laughed and ran up to her father. "I'm going to like living here!"

Mrs. Greer, the woman who ran the boarding house, was very friendly. "I'm afraid all we have left is one small room at the top of the house. But that shouldn't be a problem for a champion runner like you," she said, nodding at Keeley's medal.

They climbed the sets of stairs to the small room at the top of the house. It was a tiny place with sloping walls. They were right underneath the roof.

"The main chimney runs up through here, so it will give you some heat in the winter," Mrs. Greer said. "There's only room for one bed, but look over here."

A dormer window in the corner created a little alcove. "There's just enough room for us to build a window seat for you to sleep on," she said to Keeley. "It will be just your size, as long as you don't grow too much too fast."

"I won't grow," Keeley promised. The window was the highest spot in town. The only thing higher was the mountain.

Mrs. Greer knelt down by Keeley to look out the window with her.

"The Kootenay Indians live all over this area," she said, "but they never camp around here. They never have. They say Turtle Mountain is restless, that it will get up and move one day."

Keeley looked out at the great mass of rock and earth. "How can a mountain move?"

"I don't know, but you can be the town lookout. Keep an eye on the mountain, and if it starts to go anywhere, let us know."

"How will I do that?"

"Open the window and yell out, 'The mountain is moving!'"

"I can do that," Keeley replied. "I like to yell."

Mrs. Greer and Pop talked adult talk, while Keeley leaned out the window and looked at the people on the street below. Living here would be fun.

Keeley and Pop had just enough time to fetch their belongings from the train station luggage

room and get to the meadow before the celebration began.

They sat with nine hundred other people at
the long outdoor tables. They feasted on fried
chicken, salad, and fresh bread and butter. More
men made more speeches, but everyone was too
busy eating to listen.

"I see some other men with their job papers,"
Pop said to Keeley when the first course was
over. "I'm going to introduce myself."

"But dessert is coming—it's ice cream."

"I'll be back before it melts." He left the table.

Keeley waited with admirable patience for the
ice cream and fruit salad, but when it finally
came, there was no Pop.

This will melt fast, she thought. I'd better take
it to him. Not wanting her own dessert to melt,
she picked up both bowls and went in search of
her father.

She was walking beside one of the long tables
when something caught her leg. She sprawled
onto the grass. The ice cream bowls flew out of

her hands. Keeley, her face on the ground, didn't see where they landed.

She felt someone else's leg underneath her and grabbed it quickly. Someone had tripped her, and she was going to find out who.

"Let go of my leg!"

Keeley looked at the leg's owner. It was Peter, the boy she had beaten in the foot race.

"You tripped me," she said.

"I didn't trip you. You were just walking with your nose in the air."

"And you made me drop my ice cream." Keeley let go of the boy's leg and got up off the ground. She brushed herself off. "Where is my ice cream?"

Keeley became aware of the gasps of the people around them. She looked up and froze at the horror that greeted her eyes. The bowls full of ice cream and fruit had sailed through the air and landed *kerplop* on a woman seated at the table. One bowl was in her lap. The other was on her head. The ice cream and fruit dripped down over her face, covering it completely.

Someone handed the woman a towel. She wiped the ice cream away.

Keeley's horror grew as the towel revealed none other than the sour-faced woman whose hat Keeley had pulled off on the train. The woman stared right at Keeley. She was not pleased.

"If I were you, I'd run," Peter said, laughing.

Keeley ran without looking where she was going. She bumped into someone, who bumped into someone else. As she ran, she heard tables collapsing and people hollering.

I have to find Pop, she thought as she ran. We have to get out of town before anyone realizes who I am and what I've done.

"Ooof!" Keeley ran smack into someone. It was her father. "Pop!" she exclaimed.

"Come with me, Keeley. I have a surprise for you."

Pop led Keeley away from the chaos she had created and up the steps of the platform where she had received her medal. "Here she is," Pop said to one of the whiskered men.

"Meet Keeley O'Brien, who will from now on also be known as Little Miss Frank."

"Ladies and gentlemen, may I have your attention?" The whiskered man shouted into the microphone. "We have here a little girl who shares the same birthday as our new town. I want you all to know who she is. Meet Keeley O'Brien, who will from now on also be known as Little Miss Frank."

A wide sash was put over Keeley's shoulder. "Careful, the paint is still wet." Keeley looked down and saw the words *Little Miss Frank* spread across her chest. Someone stuck a bunch of wildflowers in her hand.

"And now let's all sing 'Happy Birthday' to our birthday girl and to our new town of Frank."

Feeling very uncomfortable, Keeley stood on the platform while nine hundred people sang to her. She tried not to look at the back tables, where the people she had knocked over were trying to get the food off their clothes and out of their hair.

CHAPTER N°. 5

"Wake up, sleepyhead."

A pleasant voice pushed its way into Keeley's sleeping brain. Keeley chose to ignore it and kept sleeping.

"Wake up!" The woman's voice was more impatient this time.

I'm tired, Keeley thought, keeping her eyes closed.

"Get up now, or I'll call the doc to come and dose you with cod liver oil!"

That got Keeley up. Her grandmother had been a big believer in cod liver oil.

"Who are you?" Keeley rubbed her eyes and looked at the young woman frowning down at her, hands crossed across her apron front.

"I'm Lillian Clark. I work here, and you are not going to hold me up in the mornings. Understand?"

"Where's my pop?"

"Gone to work. What did you expect, that he could just wander into the mine whenever he felt like it? Things are done on a schedule in the mine, just as they are in this boarding house, and I won't stand for you putting me behind schedule."

"You don't need to be so grouchy," Keeley said, getting up off the mat on the floor she'd slept on. The carpenter hadn't built her bed yet. "Mrs. Greer isn't grouchy."

"Mrs. Greer has her moments. And your father put me in charge of you, so you'd better do what I say."

"School doesn't start for a week yet. I can sleep in if I want to."

Lillian and Keeley gave each other a good hard stare. "I'm going down to put your oatmeal on the kitchen table," Lillian said as she left the room. "If it's cold by the time you get down there, it will be your own fault."

Keeley was dressed and ready in minutes, having experienced the horror of cold oatmeal too many times in her life already. She opened the door and headed downstairs.

The stairs stopped at the first landing, and Keeley opened the door into a long hallway of closed doors. She looked one way, then the other, but couldn't remember which direction to go. She'd been too excited to pay attention the first time she'd come up, and she was too tired last night.

All the doors looked the same. "I'll just start opening them," she said to herself. "One will lead to the stairs that will get me to my oatmeal before it gets cold and gluey."

The first door wouldn't open. She rattled the handle, and a gruff man's voice shouted out, "Go away!" The second door opened, but it was just an empty bedroom, none too tidy.

"It's like a treasure hunt," she said. She flung wide the third door—and immediately wished she hadn't.

A beautiful woman with bright red hair in great swirls around her head was sitting at a table with a man in his shirt sleeves and suspenders. They were drinking something from china cups.

"Scram, kid," the man growled.

Keeley was about to scram when something caught her eye. "That looks like one of my mother's paintings," she said, walking into the bedroom to look at the painting of a flowered landscape that hung on the wall. The woman's perfume was sweet, like the flowers.

"Your mother is a painter?" the woman asked, ignoring the man's sputtering. She stood behind Keeley, looking at the painting.

"She was. She's dead, but I still have some of her paintings. Would you like to see them?"

"Yes, I would." The woman's voice was kind. Keeley turned around to look at her. Her face was kind, too. She wore a tight purple corset that shimmered in the morning light. A lacy black robe hung from her shoulders. "I used to like to paint when I was a girl."

"Why did you stop?"

"I don't have any paint." This seemed to give her an idea. "Harvey, get me a set of paints and some brushes while you're in Vancouver, will you? You wanted to get me a present. That's what I'd like. Harvey is a friend of mine," she explained.

Keeley introduced herself. Harvey made some strange noises. Keeley decided that was his way of saying hello.

"I'm Violet," the woman said.

"Like the flower," Keeley said, smiling, then she remembered her breakfast. "I have to get to the kitchen before my oatmeal gets cold, but I can't find the way down."

Violet wrapped her robe around her corset, took Keeley out into the hall, and showed her which door led to the kitchen stairs. They made plans to meet again later, after Harvey left for Vancouver, to look at the paintings.

Keeley's oatmeal was a bit cold and gluey, but she poured molasses and cream on it, and it tasted all right.

"Your father asked me to remind you to write a letter to your grandparents," Mrs. Greer said, coming into the kitchen as Keeley was helping herself to a piece of bread and blackberry jam.

"I hate writing letters," Keeley replied.

"Don't tell me; tell your father," Mrs. Greer said. "But if you change your mind, there is paper on the desk in the parlour. I'll get the handyman to build your bed this morning. You'll want to unpack and get settled."

"You have some nice people staying here," Keeley said. "I met Violet this morning by accident when I was looking for the stairs to the kitchen. She's going to look at the paintings."

Mrs. Greer stopped on her way out the back door. "I don't know that your father will think that's a very good idea," she said.

"Pop won't mind. He loves it when people see what a great painter my mother was."

Mrs. Greer opened her mouth as if to say something else, then changed her mind. "It's none of my business," she said, which Keeley didn't understand but didn't worry about.

After breakfast, Keeley dutifully wrote to her grandparents, telling them about her father's job and their new home. It took her longer than it should have because she didn't enjoy letter writing, and she wasted a lot of time sighing and wiggling in her chair. But at least it was done.

Just as she was folding the paper, Violet and Harvey passed by the parlour on their way to the front door. Keeley waited patiently while they said goodbye to each other. "Remember the paints," she heard Violet call out.

"Can I see your mother's paintings now?" she asked Keeley. Keeley didn't need to be asked twice. She ran up the stairs with Violet close behind. The little room at the top of the house smelled pleasantly of fresh wood—the handyman had finished building Keeley's bed. Keeley got the bundle of paintings from the corner of the room, and she and Violet sat on her new bed.

Keeley's fingers trembled as she tried to undo the knot in the cloth that kept the package closed. Violet gently took it from her and opened it. Keeley spread apart the layers of cloth until the paintings were revealed. She didn't realize she was crying until Violet wiped her tears away. "I'd forgotten how beautiful they are. My grandparents didn't let me display them. They only liked religious pictures."

Violet picked up the paintings and looked closely at them. "They are absolutely beautiful."

"My mother's own parents didn't like her painting things, either. She had to learn to paint in secret. That's why they're so small."

Violet spread them out on the bed. There were six paintings, not much bigger than one of Keeley's copybooks. They were in rubbed wood frames her father had made. The colours made them seem

41

bigger, strong, and delicate at the same time. Keeley remembered her mother's hand holding the paintbrush, making tiny strokes over and over until the canvas glowed with colour and life.

"I don't understand your grandparents, Keeley," Violet said. "There is plenty of religion in these, just like there is in nature. I wish I could create something so beautiful."

Keeley knew then that she would always, always love Violet.

They spent the rest of the morning deciding where the paintings should go. Hanging them on the walls made the little room feel like home.

Violet spread them out on the bed. There were six paintings, not much bigger than one of Keeley's copybooks.

CHAPTER N° 6

After lunch, Keeley went off on an errand for Mrs. Greer. She carried a reed basket lined with soft cloths.

"Go to the edge of town," Mrs. Greer said, pointing her in the right direction, "then keep on going, until you think you've gone too far. Then go a bit farther. You'll know it when you see it. I won't tell you any more. I don't want to spoil the surprise."

"What if I get lost?"

"And what if you don't? Women have to be independent out here. You might as well start learning how."

Keeley walked and walked, following a path beside the Oldman River.

In a clearing by a bend in the river a hairy old man was stretched out on the ground, snoring in the warmth of the afternoon. Nearby was a tent, a fire pit, and some rough-hewn wood furniture. Keeley hurried by so she wouldn't wake him. She hoped he would be still sleeping when she had to come back.

Finally, she got to where she was going.

"Honey House" was the name carved into the little archway over the gate. The yard was full of huge wood carvings, some of animals Keeley could recognize, others of shapes she had never seen before. It looked like an enchanted forest out of a fairy tale.

Keeley walked slowly up the pathway. The fall wildflowers were in full bloom. Keeley felt as if she were inside one of her mother's paintings.

"Who are you?"

Keeley turned around at the sound of the woman's voice, then let out a screech. The woman—or whatever it was—had no face, just a strange helmet in place of a head. "Don't make such an ugly noise on such a pretty day. Tell me your name," the strange creature said.

Keeley could only screech again, especially when the creature came closer and tried to put a giant hand on her shoulder.

"Mable—take that hat off. No wonder the child is scared."

Out of the house came another woman wearing men's dungarees and carrying an axe. Her hair was white and roughly cut.

"Oh, goodness, I forgot I had it on." Mable reached up and patted the giant hat-thing with her giant gloves. First she took the gloves off, then she pulled off the giant hat-thing, revealing that she did indeed have a human head and quite a nice face, even though it was covered with sweat. "I spend so much time with the bees, I forget how to act around people." She laughed, a great laugh that bounced off the mountain and swirled around the valley.

"Patricia!" the axe-carrying woman called out, with very able lungs. "That's our granddaughter. She's off in her tree, I imagine. You should meet her. She's just your age."

"I'm Mable," said the other woman, "and this is Ethel."

Ethel came down the pathway and held out her axe. "Oops, forgive me." She transferred the axe to her other hand and gave Keeley a vigorous handshake. "Do you like my sculptures?"

"I don't understand all of them," Keeley said truthfully.

"Splendid!" said Ethel. "What good is understanding everything? If we understood everything, we'd never get out of bed because there would be nothing to look forward to. What brings you out here?"

Keeley raised her basket. "Mrs. Greer at the boarding house sent me. She said you'd know what for."

"Honey," said Mable, taking the basket. "Go down that path and climb the biggest tree you see. I'll send snacks to you in a jiffy."

The two women went inside the house, leaving Keeley with nothing to do but what she was told. The pathway went around the little house, past the big vegetable garden that was laid out like a wheel, and into a little thicket of trees. The biggest tree was easy to spot, but there was a Keep Out sign at the bottom.

"It's all right. You can come up."

Keeley looked up. A little face with big round glasses peered down at her from a house in the branches. "Hey—you're the girl from the saloon!" A rope ladder came swinging down at her. Keeley wasn't sure it was safe, but gave it a try anyway. It swayed as she climbed it, but she hung on and kept climbing.

"I'm Keeley," she said when she got to the top.

"Pull the ladder up behind you," the girl said, then introduced herself. "I'm Patricia. That was a good fight the other day." Patricia was shuffling some playing cards.

"Are there a lot of fights at the saloon?" Keeley

asked, rolling up the ladder as she pulled it up.

"Well, I'm not there every day, but when I'm there, there's usually something going on. I haven't seen anybody get shot yet, though." Patricia's glasses slipped a little on her nose, and she pushed them back up on her face.

"I haven't seen anybody get shot, either. I don't think I'd like to."

"I would," Patricia said. "It would be something different. It's good to see lots of different things, instead of the same old thing all the time."

That's probably true, Keeley thought, but she still didn't think she'd want to see somebody shot.

Keeley's eyes went from Patricia to the tree-house. It was shaped to fit perfectly into the nest made by the spread of the tree. The treehouse boards had strange carvings on them. Keeley took a closer look. "That's you!" she exclaimed.

"That's me, and there's my mother and father—they're dead—and here's Grandma Mable and here's Grandma Ethel. Well, Grandma Mable is my real grandmother. Ethel is her friend. It's just easier to call them both Grandma. Grandma Ethel made the treehouse. Would you like to play some blackjack?"

Patricia taught Keeley how to play, and they were deep into the game when a bell rang. Patricia stood up and went to the side of the treehouse. A box was swinging its way toward them on a rope that stretched all the way to the main house. Patricia grabbed it and put it on the floor of the treehouse. She took out a jar of cold tea, two glasses and some cookies.

"Don't look so surprised," she said. "It's snack time."

The cookies had bits of dried apple in them. Keeley leaned back against a cushion while she munched. "Do you ever sleep up here?" she asked.

"Sure. That's what treehouses are for. I sleep on the mountain sometimes, too."

"By yourself?"

"With my grandmothers. They know all the good sleeping spots. Do you want to come with us sometime?"

"Can my father come, too?"

"Is he a yeller? I don't like yelly men."

Keeley laughed. "Pop is a poet. He works in the mine. He doesn't have to yell to do either of those things."

"Then he can come with us."

Keeley was sent back to the boarding house late that afternoon with two pottery jars of honey in her basket and a packet of cookies to drop off to the old man who camped out by the river. "His name is Andy Grissick. He's an old trapper, lives by the river in that tent all year round, sun or snow," Mable said. "He's harmless, so don't let his looks scare you. The worst thing he'll do is bend your ear with those tall tales of his."

"They're not tall tales," Ethel said.

"Don't rely on Ethel's judgment," Mable said. "She still believes in fairies."

Keeley found it hard to believe that muscular Ethel, who carried an axe with the same ease her own grandmother carried a darning needle, could ever believe in anything as delicate as fairies, but Ethel confirmed it. "I see them dancing around my statues sometimes when the moon is full."

Back at the boarding house, Mrs. Greer took the basket of honey from her. "Did you like the surprise?"

Keeley thought for a minute before answering. There was something she had been thinking about, and she wanted to get it right. Then she had it. "People can choose to be just whoever they want to be out here, can't they?"

"They sure can," Mrs. Greer said. "So be careful what you choose."

Pop was covered in coal dust when he got home from the mine. Keeley, waiting in front of the boarding house, could hardly recognize him.

"Smile so I know it's you," she said.

Pop growled like a monster and chased her around the yard.

"Stop! Stop!" she squealed, out of breath. "Pop, I met a lady in the boarding house this morning.

Her name is Violet. She helped me hang Mom's paintings. Come and see."

There were several other miners who stayed at the boarding house. Pop joined them at the pump. "Let me get some of the mine off me first," he said.

Mrs. Greer had left old rags out by the pump for the miners to use. The rags were clean but grey from all the coal dust that had rubbed off on them. Pop scrubbed until his hands and face were their usual colour, perhaps a little redder from the chilly water.

"Come and see," Keeley said again.

"I'll race you," Pop said. They sped into the house, up the back stairs, and into the little room at the top.

Pop stopped and looked around. "It's just like she was here with us," he said. "You and your friend Violet did a wonderful job."

"Would you like to meet her?" Keeley didn't wait for an answer. She grabbed Pop's hand and pulled him down the stairs. She knocked on only one wrong door before she found the right one.

Violet had changed out of her corset and was wearing a blue frock with lots of frills and flounces.

"You're beautiful!" Keeley said. "This is my father."

Pop told Violet his name and bowed slightly as they shook hands. Keeley watched them smile at each other. Keeley loved the way her pop was always a gentleman, even when his clothes were covered in coal dust.

CHAPTER 7

"Good morning, mountain." Keeley stretched herself awake. The mountain looked down at her through her window. It hadn't moved during the night.

There was a quick, sharp knock at the door, and Lillian put her head inside the room. "Time to get up, Keeley. You don't want to be late on the first day of school."

"Yes, I do. I want to be very, very late. I want to be so late that school is over by the time I get there."

"You're lucky to be going to school. Wait until

you start working. You'll realize how much fun school was."

Keeley had realized by now that Lillian was always grouchy first thing in the morning. But by the time the day was halfway over, Lillian was halfway cheerful.

Lillian left Keeley to get ready. Pop started work at seven in the morning and had to be at the mine even earlier, so he got up long before Keeley. He also liked to go for a walk before going to the mine, to get as much fresh air in his lungs as he could before going underground. Keeley hardly saw him most mornings.

She considered staying cozily in her bed, but since Pop counted on her to get up, she got up.

Keeley got dressed and hurried down to breakfast. Other tenants were at breakfast, too, so she ate with them in the big dining room. "Where's Violet?" she asked, noticing her friend wasn't there.

Some of the adults made funny noises. "Violet usually sleeps later than this," Mrs. Greer said, placing a bowl of oatmeal in front of Keeley.

"I'm surprised you let her stay here," one of the men who was not a mine worker said.

"Violet pays her rent and minds her own business, which is more than I can say for some of my lodgers," Mrs. Greer said, which put an end to the discussion.

There was a strange moment of silence, which was broken by Mr. Collins, one of the bookkeepers for the mine. "Well, Keeley, ready for the first day of school?" He smiled at her over his coffee.

"Not really."

"You're not scared, are you? A bright girl like you."

Mr. Stewart, one of the miners on the night shift, mopped up the egg yolk on his plate with a hunk of Mrs. Greer's homemade bread.

"Of course she's not scared," Mrs. Greer said. "Keeley's not afraid of anything. You eat all that oatmeal, Keeley. It will give you strength."

Mrs. Greer believed in large portions. The bowl of oatmeal seemed bottomless. Keeley was saved from finishing it when Mrs. Greer noticed the time.

"Off you go," she said.

"Isn't anybody going with me?"

"You know where the school is," Mrs. Greer said. "Independence, remember?" Keeley remembered. It wasn't that she was shy; it was just that . . . well, maybe she *was* shy.

"I have lots of time," Keeley said to herself. "There's no point in hurrying and then just having to stand around before the bell rings."

After being in Frank for a week, Keeley knew her way around town. She knew a lot of the townspeople, too, and a lot of people knew her. Not everyone knew her name, but they did recognize her as Little Miss Frank. Usually she liked being well-known. This morning, though, everyone she saw reminded her not to be late for school.

Keeley left the main street and walked by the stable.

"What happened to Charlie?"

Mr. Watt, the stable boss, was wrapping a bandage around the fetlock of Keeley's favourite mine horse. She had met him on an evening walk with her father to the mouth of the mine. Charlie had been pulling a wagon full of coal out of the mine on tracks that looked like small train tracks.

"He was hit with a piece of coal that jumped unexpectedly out of the mountain," Mr. Watt said. "But I've cleaned the cut, and we'll let him rest for a few days. He'll be fine."

"You deserve a rest, don't you, Charlie?" Keeley stroked Charlie's soft brown nose. "Hauling all those heavy wagons of coal every day can't be good for you."

"You'd better hurry, Keeley," Mr. Watt said, tying one last knot in the bandage. "You don't want to be late for the first day of school."

"I won't be late," Keeley replied politely. For a moment, she wished she were back in Lethbridge, where everybody minded their own business.

Keeley gave Charlie a quick kiss and continued on her way, but still without hurrying. She tossed sticks for Dexter, the little terrier who lived in the house next door to the stable. She was in mid-throw when the school bell rang.

"Oh, no—I'm going to be late!" Keeley started to run.

Dexter, thinking it was part of the game, ran after her with the stick in his mouth. He attracted the attention of the two neighbour dogs, who joined in the fun.

Keeley kept running, her eyes focused ahead of her. When she got to the schoolhouse, there wasn't a person in sight.

Up the steps and into the building she ran. Maybe the class hadn't started yet, and the teacher wouldn't notice she was late.

Keeley flung open the door, burst inside—and froze. A roomful of children stopped singing the national anthem and stared at her.

The first thing Keeley realized was that the dogs had followed her into the school and were now barking with joy and jumping on the students.

The second thing she realized was that a boy was standing at the front of the class, leading the morning exercises, and that the boy was Peter— the same boy who had tripped her and tried to rob her of her first-place medal.

"Don't tell me you're the teacher," Keeley shouted above the noise of the barking and the laughing kids. "What fool put you in charge of the class?"

The laughter stopped. Even the dogs stopped barking. Everyone's attention was focused on a spot just behind Keeley.

Keeley turned around and wanted to fall through the floor.

The third thing she realized, and the worst, was that the teacher was the sour-faced woman from the train, the one who had worn Keeley's ice cream for a hat.

The teacher's eyes widened with horror at the sight of Keeley, but only for a moment. She quickly regained her teacherlike composure and pointed without speaking to an empty chair at

The first thing Keeley realized
was that the dogs had followed
her into the school and were
now barking with joy and
jumping on the students.

a double desk near the front of the girls' side of the room. Keeley went where she was directed. By some miracle, her seat partner was Patricia. At least something was going right this morning!

At another swoop of the teacher's finger, Peter gathered up the dogs, took them outside, and was back at his desk within minutes.

"I am Miss Griffin," the teacher said. The class sang "God Save the King," recited the Lord's Prayer, and the school day began.

In the schoolyard at lunch break, Keeley attracted an admiring throng.

"What a great trick, bringing in those dogs," someone said.

Patricia looped her arm through Keeley's. "It was no trick. Keeley's just brave."

"She must be," someone else said, "to do that on the first day of school."

"She's not so brave," Peter said. "She probably didn't even mean to bring the dogs. It was prob- ably an accident."

"It was not an accident," Keeley lied, her honour at stake. "You only think so because you'd never be brave enough to do anything like that."

"Oh, yeah? Well, if it wasn't an accident, I dare you to do it again."

"I never repeat the same trick," Keeley said grandly. "That would bore me."

"Yeah, that would bore her," the girls echoed. They surrounded Keeley and walked with her out of the schoolyard.

Keeley was kept in after class that afternoon to write on the blackboard one hundred times that she would not be late for class again. By the time she was finished, she didn't feel quite so brave. Mostly, she felt foolish. She kept expecting Miss Griffin to bring up the accident with the ice cream and the incident on the train, but Miss Griffin didn't say a word.

CHAPTER N.º 8

Peter wouldn't let up.

"No dogs today?" he'd say every morning. "What a surprise."

"I'd do it again if I wanted to," Keeley replied. "I just don't want to."

"You're all talk," he jeered. The other boys backed him up. "Talk, talk, talk. Yak, yak, yak. You're just a Big Yak."

Keeley wasn't entirely sure what a yak was, but it didn't sound good. She looked it up in the classroom dictionary. A yak was a wild long-haired ox that lived in Tibet.

"You can't let him get away with that," Patricia said, reading over her shoulder.

"He's not getting away with anything," Keeley stated. Her face was grim and determined. All through the rest of the school day, she thought of a plan.

She put her plan into action that night.

She had to keep herself awake until the rest of the house was quiet and Pop was snoring. If he woke up when she was leaving the room, she planned to say she was going down to the lavatory, but she was in luck—he kept snoring. She had worn her clothes under her nightgown; now she picked up her shoes and her jacket and left the bedroom. She got downstairs without being caught, but had to duck down into some shadows just as Mrs. Greer went through the hallway from the kitchen, where she'd been giving the loaves one last punch before putting them in pans, ready for baking in the morning.

Keeley was glad she'd taken the precaution of putting some pillows under her bedcovers, just in case Pop woke up and looked over to check on her.

Keeley was surprised at how quickly her eyes grew used to the darkness. Without any difficulty, she went into the backyard of the boarding house. Mrs. Greer kept a few goats and chickens. Keeley borrowed one of the goats, left the yard, and headed for the school.

The town was asleep. Keeley and the goat had to duck into a shadow to avoid Constable Leard on patrol. She clasped her hand over the goat's mouth, and the officer passed by without noticing them.

Keeley let out the deep breath she'd been holding in and smiled. This was going to be easy. Then she turned around and almost screamed.

Ethel was standing in the alley, blocking her way. "Hello, Keeley," she said pleasantly. "Do you like looking at shadows, too?"

"I, uh—"

"I like to walk at night and look at the shapes of shadows. Gives me ideas for my sculptures. Look over here." She pointed to strange shadowy shapes across the street. "Wonderful shapes. Could I carve that? I wonder." She took another look at Keeley, who was clutching tightly at the goat. "Are you about to do something you're not supposed to do?"

Keeley saw no way out. She nodded.

"You don't look warm enough to be getting into trouble." Ethel took off the long woollen scarf she had draped around her neck and wrapped it around Keeley. "That's much better. Now, don't let me hold you up." Ethel stepped aside so Keeley could go by. "Have fun," she called after Keeley in a whisper.

This town sure is a strange place, Keeley thought. She passed by Ethel through the alley and came out behind the main street.

The schoolyard was empty. The goat grew stubborn at the bottom of the stairs, and Keeley had to play a game of tug-of-war to get it into the schoolroom. The goat kept getting distracted, trying to chew on the end of Ethel's scarf. At last she dragged it inside and closed the door. She hurried back to the boarding house and giggled the rest of the night.

"What's that smell?"

A terrible odour hit the children as soon as they walked into the school the next morning.

Miss Griffin was waiting for them. So was the goat. It looked quite proud of itself as it chewed away on what was left of the teacher's desk blotter.

"Does anyone know whose goat this is?" she asked.

No one answered.

"Well, then, since I found it, I guess I'll keep it. Robert, please take it to the butcher's for me. I have no place to keep a goat, but I do like goat meat."

"Wait," Keeley said. "It looks awfully familiar. I could be wrong, but I think it's one of Mrs. Greer's goats."

"And how did it get here from the boarding house?"

Keeley shrugged her shoulders.

"In that case, I must assume that Mrs. Greer is up to some criminal mischief in her spare time, although I would have thought that running a boarding house would keep her busy enough. Robert, please go fetch the constable. We shall have to bring charges against Mrs. Greer."

"Wait!" Keeley spoke up again. "Maybe it just walked here by itself. Maybe Mrs. Greer didn't have anything to do with it."

"If you have something to say, Keeley O'Brien, you had better say it."

Keeley looked down at the floor. "I brought the goat into the class. It was a dare."

"Owning up to it shows you have some smidgen of redeemable character within you somewhere. I won't ask you to reveal who dared you to do such a foolish thing, because it doesn't matter. The classroom is foul and will need to be cleaned before any lessons can take place."

Miss Griffin pointed a finger, and within minutes the students were fetching buckets of water and scrubbing.

She made them clean all morning. She even made them wash the windows, which the goat couldn't possibly have soiled. "You will all come back to class on Saturday morning to make up for the lessons you missed today, " she announced.

There was plenty of grumbling in the school-yard when the class broke for lunch.

"All for some stupid prank," the kids said to Keeley. "I hope you're sorry."

Keeley refused to apologize. She went right up to Peter, put her face two inches from his, and said, "Who's the Big Yak now?"

"Yak, yak, yak!" Patricia led the girls in taunting the boys, then everyone hurried off for lunch.

CHAPTER N.º 9

Not even Pop's lecture and Keeley's extra chores at the boarding house to make up for the trouble she had caused Mrs. Greer were enough to stem the tide of dares.

Peter was eager to get rid of the title of Big Yak. At Keeley's dare, he stole a frying pan from Andy Grissick, the craggy old trapper who lived in a tent by the Oldman River. He balanced the pan in the fork of the tree that sheltered Mr. Grissick's campsite.

"Yak, yak," he said to Keeley, who was watching from some bushes.

In return, Keeley had to go into the lobby of the Palm Restaurant during the busy lunch hour. She had to stand in the middle of the restaurant and sing "God Save the King" at the top of her voice.

She was almost ready to let Peter win. When she walked into the restaurant, all the grown-ups at the tables looked very big, and very busy with their food. They would not like being interrupted.

"Go on," Peter said behind her. He gave her a little shove between the shoulder blades. "Stand right in the middle. And remember, it has to be loud."

Keeley stumbled forward to a space in the centre of the restaurant.

I can do this, she thought. It's just a song.

She squared her shoulders, stared at the chalk-board advertising the blue plate special, and sang right to it.

The first two lines were lost in the din, then people started to listen. Before she was a quarter of the way through the song, diners had pushed back their chairs, napkins still tucked under their chins, and were standing at attention. Some men even put their hands over their hearts.

Keeley sang the last line, there was brief applause, then everyone went back to their steaks and baked beans.

Keeley bolted for the door, but was stopped by Violet, who was having lunch with one of her gentlemen friends. "You have a lovely singing voice, Keeley," Violet said.

Keeley bent down to whisper. "Don't tell my pop," she pleaded. "I did it on a dare, and I'm not supposed to do things like that."

"I won't tell," Violet promised, "but your father will probably find out from someone else. Frank is growing, but it's still a small town. People talk."

"Keep your fingers crossed for me that no one tells him."

Violet held up her hands, fingers crossed, and nudged her luncheon companion to do the same. Keeley grinned and went outside to gloat to Peter.

Violet was right. Pop did find out. They were on their evening walk, and nearly everyone they ran across complimented Keeley on her singing or on her patriotism. "I can see why the town named you Little Miss Frank," someone said. "You must be very proud of her," they said to Pop.

Pop admitted that he was proud, but as soon as they were alone again, he asked Keeley, "Was there some sort of school concert today?"

Keeley told him about the dare. "The really funny part was that when I started to sing, everyone put down their forks and stood at attention."

"I thought I told you to stop all this daring nonsense."

"Pop, I can't stop just yet. Peter and the boys will win if I do."

"Keeley, we may be living in this town for a good long time. Once you get a reputation as a troublemaker, it's hard to shake."

"It's just a game, Pop. And I've already promised you that we won't take anyone else's property or do things that will get anyone else in trouble."

"Promise me also that you won't do anything dangerous."

"But what if Peter dares me to?"

"Tell him your pop said no. Keeley, if I can't trust you to act with sense, I'll have to send you back to your grandparents'."

Keeley promised to act with sense. She'd just have to be more creative in thinking up dares for Peter.

She and Patricia spent long hours in the tree-house, talking and scheming. The dare they came up with for Peter was, to use Patricia's word, a masterpiece.

"Change the sign on the photography studio," she dared him. "It now reads 'Our photographs will always whisper, Come Again.' Make it read 'Our photographs will always whisper, Go Away!'"

The shop window was always full of scary-looking photographs of ugly ladies and gentle-men. The new slogan made much more sense.

"How am I supposed to do that?"

Keeley shrugged. "Yak, yak" was all she said.

Early Sunday morning, Keeley and Peter met outside the boarding house and headed up Dominion Street. Peter carried a can of paint and a brush.

Keeley took up a lookout position beside the whiskey store across the street. This early, there was no one about.

"This is too easy," she decided. "I should have made him do it on a Saturday afternoon."

"Good morning," a man said. Keeley jumped, trying to think up an excuse for being out so early.

She didn't need one. The young man didn't seem to think there was anything strange in her behaviour.

"Which do you think is better?" he asked her. He had a sign he was going to attach to the door of a small shop beside the whiskey store. He moved the sign up and down the door.

"Up a little higher," she said, then read the sign. "What's a Frank Sentinal?"

"Newspaper," the man replied. He held out his free hand for Keeley to shake. "Harry Matheson, owner, publisher, and sole reporter of the new town newspaper."

Keeley shook Mr. Matheson's hand. "I know another reporter," she said, "a woman. Her name is Cora Hind. Do you know her?"

"I certainly know of her." He looked around for his hammer and nails.

Keeley took a closer look at the sign. "I think *Sentinal* is spelled wrong. It's *el*, not *al*.

"Are you sure?"

"Spelling's just about the only subject I'm good at."

"Spelling's not my subject at all," Harry said. "If you ever want a job . . . Uh-oh, somebody's in trouble." He nodded down the street.

Keeley looked and groaned. She was supposed to be the lookout. She should have been paying attention.

Constable Leard was standing over Peter. Keeley couldn't hear what he was saying, but whenever grown-ups put their hands on their hips, it usually meant they were up to no good.

Harry looked at Keeley's expression of horror and started to laugh. "I'll bet there's a good story there."

Keeley didn't find the situation nearly so funny.

CHAPTER N.º 10

"In you go," Peter said. *"And don't come* out until the morning."

"And don't let yourself get caught, either," Sean, Peter's friend, said. "There are lots of hiding places off the opening tunnel. If you get caught, it's because you want to be, because you're scared."

"Keeley, don't do this," Patricia urged. "The mine is dangerous. I took the tour on the first day, and the mine men said over and over again that a mine is dangerous, and people should not just wander in. Even my grandmothers won't let me go in there, and they let me do everything. Besides, your father will be furious."

"He'll never know—unless you tell him," Peter said. "In you go. The night is speeding by. And don't try to come out early. We'll be back here first thing in the morning. If we don't see you come out then, we'll know you were too scared to stay. And you know what that means!"

"Yak, yak," said Sean.

The four children were standing a short ways from the mine entrance. Peter's dare to Keeley was that she should spend a night in the mine.

"If you want me to go in there with you, I will," Patricia offered.

Keeley couldn't allow that. She'd be in enough trouble for going in by herself. She didn't want the added problem of having someone else get into trouble with her. "No, the dare is to do it alone."

"How will she know when it's morning?" Patricia asked. "It's dark in the mine all the time."

"She can come out after the miners change shift."

Keeley took a tighter grip on her bundle. "Sleep well," she told them. "I know I will."

"Unless you get eaten by a mountain lion," Peter jeered.

"Only an idiot like you would think that mountain lions lived in mines," Keeley retorted to cover up her fear. She hadn't considered mountain lions.

Sometimes miners came out of the tunnel to eat their mid-shift meal. Keeley checked to make sure the coast was clear, then left the shelter of the bushes and followed the tracks into the mouth of the mine.

The mine shaft was dug straight into the side of Turtle Mountain. Keeley could hear the noise of the miners far in the distance chipping away at the coal in the mountain's stomach. She felt better knowing her father was among them. He was working the night shift tonight. Keeley had been allowed to sleep over at Patricia's house. That made it easy for them to sneak out together.

Small gas lamps gave off a bit of light, making giant spooky shadows along the sides and roof of the tunnel. The only thing that kept Keeley from dashing back outside was the triumphant look that would be on Peter's face. "Ethel should see these shadows," she said. "They'd give her lots of ideas for sculptures." Her voice sounded strange, bouncing off the rock.

A smaller tunnel opened up off the main one. Before going down it, Keeley lit the candle she had brought with her in her pocket.

The little tunnel didn't lead anywhere. It just stopped after fifty feet.

"This will make a lovely home." Keeley spoke out loud to try to cheer herself up.

She put her candle in a niche in the wall and unwrapped the blankets that held the bundle together.

She had a jar of cold tea, a jam sandwich, and three of Mrs. Greer's oatmeal raisin cookies. She also had an old flour sack to fold up and use as a pillow. She didn't think Mrs. Greer would want her to take one of the boarding house pillows into the mine.

"I'll pretend this is my bedroom in one of the little cottages," she said. "I'll make my bed here by the pretend window, so I can look out and see what the weather is like without leaving the covers."

She put her lunch on a little rock shelf she called her kitchen. Then she wrapped herself up in her blankets and lay down on her flour sack pillow. The ground was hard, and she missed her window-seat bed.

"I wish I'd brought another candle," she whispered. Then she closed her eyes and fell asleep.

Keeley's bed started to shake. In her sleepy state, she thought at first she was back on the train, rolling into Frank.

But wait a minute—she wasn't on the train! She was inside the mountain, and the mountain was shaking!

Keeley sat up, opening her eyes just seconds before the candle was shaken from its niche in the wall. It fell to the ground and sputtered out.

"Help!" Keeley yelled in a panic. She ran towards what she thought was the way out, but thumped straight into a wall instead.

The shaking got worse. With a noise that sounded like the mountain screaming, a gush of rocks and dust slammed down around Keeley.

She didn't know how long she screamed and waved her arms. She had to stop to catch her breath. The air she took in was full of dust, but it calmed her down.

Keeley dropped to her knees, found the blankets, and wrapped them around her. She instantly felt better, as if the blankets could somehow protect her.

If she could find the blankets, maybe she could find the candle and the matches, too.

Keeping close to the floor, she felt around in the darkness. She found her sandwich first and close to that the cookies and tea. The candle was almost under one of her feet. For a long while, it seemed as though the matches were gone, but at last her fingers curled around the little box.

Keeley held the candle between her feet while she lit it. The light was a blessing. She poured a bit of wax onto the floor and set the candle down into it.

She could see now that the way out of the tunnel was blocked by a big pile of rocks. Some of the rocks were small, but most were huge boulders.

Careful not to knock over the candle with the sweep of her blanket, Keeley went up to the pile to get a closer look. The ceiling in the tunnel was low. The top of the pile couldn't be very high.

She started to climb. She got a foot or two off the ground, then the rocks shifted and she slid back down again.

"Let's get rid of these," she said, tossing the blankets to the ground. Gingerly, she started to climb again.

She climbed until her head bumped up against the ceiling. Maybe if she could toss away the smaller rocks, she could make a space big enough to crawl through.

"There should be a rescue party coming," she said. "Pop has been on many rescue parties. He's probably on the other side of the pile right now, trying to get me out."

The thought occurred to Keeley that nobody knew she was there, so why would anyone be trying to dig her out? But she put that thought away. Anyway, it wasn't true. Peter knew she was in the mine. In fact, he had probably caused the rocks to fall, hoping to escape the next dare.

"He can't get out of it that easily," Keeley said. "I'll show him."

Eating her lunch would give her the energy needed to dig herself out. She sat down by the candle and ate her jam sandwich and oatmeal cookies. Mine dust was mixed with the raisins, but the cold tea washed everything down.

Fortified, she moved the candle to the back of her little space, to a niche up off the floor.

Then she tackled the rock pile.

It was hard work, flinging rocks to the ground. She slipped a lot. She could feel the sharper rocks scrape against her knees. It hurt, but she had bigger worries.

Sometimes the rock pile helped her out. She'd remove one rock and a whole bunch of other rocks would tumble down with it. Once she got knocked to the ground, hurting her arm and back.

Finally, just when Keeley thought she was too tired and sore to toss away another rock, she saw a bit of light. She rubbed her eyes with a dusty hand to be sure she was seeing properly. She was.

The light was faint, but it *was* a light. She had broken through the pile of rocks!

She tossed down the last few small rocks. All that were left were rocks too big for her to move.

"Help!" she called out through the small space. "Is anybody there? Come and get me, Pop!"

Keeley yelled a while longer, but there was no response. She could hear the mine noises deep inside the mountain. The miners were still working.

"They can't hear me," she said. "I'm never going to get out of here."

She climbed down, wrapped the blankets around her shoulders again, picked up the candle, and climbed back up the rock pile.

Keeley put the candle in the gap where someone might see its light and leaned against the rocks. She cried for a little bit, but that didn't help anything, so she stopped.

The only other thing she could think of to do was sing.

"She'll be coming 'round the mountain when she comes," she sang quietly. She sang a couple more verses, then forgot what came next, so she made up her own.

Singing made her feel braver. "I'm the bravest person in the world," she said. "I'll be written about in the newspapers. Maybe Cora Hind will even write a story about me. And if she doesn't write it properly, maybe I'll write it."

"She'll drink tea inside the mountain when she comes . . . Cora Hind will make me famous when she comes." The new verses cheered her up. She made up some more, and sang them louder because they made her happy.

"She'll throw ice cream at the teacher when she comes . . . She'll call Peter a Big Yak when she comes."

"Hey—what's that sound?"

Through her singing, Keeley heard a voice. "Help!" she yelled. "I'm in here. Pop?"

"Keeley—is that you?"

She heard the sound of running, and suddenly the little tunnel was filled with miners on the other side of the rock pile.

"Pop! Hi, Pop!"

"What are you doing in there?"

Keeley wasn't sure what to say. "Having lunch?" she ventured.

"Are you all right? Are you hurt?"

Keeley could hear rocks being pulled away.

"I'm all right."

"Stand back from the rock pile," one of the miners directed. "It could collapse while we're tossing rocks away."

Keeley did as she was told. In a short while, light from a miner's head lantern filled her little space. Pop's wonderful face was smiling at her.

"Isn't it a little bit past your bedtime?" he asked. Keeley scrambled up the rock pile, and Pop pulled her out to freedom.

He put his arms around her in one of his famous hugs. "You are in *such* big trouble," he said. Then he hugged her even harder.

CHAPTER N.º 11

Keeley, fresh from a bath, in her nightgown and wrapped in a blanket, sat in the boarding house parlour, breathing in the sweet steam of a cup of cocoa. Next to her on the sofa was Pop on one side and Violet on the other. Everyone else who lived in the boarding house was there with them.

"You must have been terribly scared," Violet said. She brushed a strand of hair off Keeley's face.

"You had no idea there had been a cave-in?" Mrs. Greer asked.

"The mountain shakes and shudders all the time," one of the other miners said. "It was

94

Keeley, fresh from a bath, in her nightgown and wrapped in a blanket, sat in the boarding house parlour, breathing in the sweet steam of a cup of cocoa.

nerve-racking at first, but now we don't even notice it anymore."

"When I think what could have happened," Pop said. "Maybe I was wrong in bringing you here. Maybe I was wrong in thinking I could take care of you. It's just by chance that we heard you singing. What if you had been knocked out? What if we hadn't heard you?" Pop's voice broke, and he pulled the blanket tighter around Keeley's shoulders.

Violet put her hand on Pop's arm. "But you did hear, and you did get her out. And she's fine."

Pop briefly covered Violet's hand with his own. "Yes, you're right. We got her out, and she's fine. Thank you for reminding me of that. I didn't lose her."

"What were you doing in the mine?" the other miner asked. "Hasn't your father told you to stay away? Mines are not playgrounds, young lady. They are not places for you to explore."

"Keeley won't have time to go exploring for a long while," Pop said. "Mrs. Greer has enough housework around here to keep Keeley nice and busy until Christmas."

"Indeed, I do," Mrs. Greer said. "Washing and ironing and all sorts of cleaning, plus dishes after every meal."

Keeley didn't even want to protest. She knew she had it coming. And helping Mrs. Greer would give her a break from the Big Yak game. She felt that she needed a rest, although she wished she could have seen Peter's face when he'd realized she had stuck it out through a cave-in, and that it was now his turn to be dared again.

"Up to bed with you, now," Pop said. "Take the cocoa with you." He gave her a hug. "If you ever do anything like that again, I'll send you back to your grandparents."

Upstairs, Keeley sat on her window-seat bed, sipping her cocoa. Turtle Mountain loomed over the town. Keeley watched it turn from black to dark grey as night slipped into early morning.

Maybe she *should* write the story about her being trapped inside the mountain. If she left it to grown-ups to write, they'd just call her experience some childish prank, instead of the act of supreme bravery that it was. Besides, writing about her adventure in a story would mean that lots and lots of people could read about it. She'd be famous for being brave, instead of for being foolish.

"You're my friend," Keeley said to the mountain. "You're big, but you don't scare me. I will camp on you with Patricia and her grandmothers. I will get to know all about you, and my pop will make us rich by taking out your coal. You're a good mountain, and we will be friends for a long, long time."

Keeley watched the light change on the mountain a while longer, until her eyelids started to droop. The excitement of the night was starting to wear off, and sleepiness was taking its place.

Something she thought she saw jerked her awake again. Had the mountain moved? No, it couldn't have. It was just a cloud passing or her lack of sleep.

Everyone knows that mountains don't move.

Canada's

1608
Samuel de Champlain establishes the first fortified trading post at Quebec.

1759
The British defeat the French in the Battle of the Plains of Abraham.

1812
The United States declares war against Canada.

1845
The expedition of Sir John Franklin to the Arctic ends when the ship is frozen in the pack ice; the fate of its crew remains a mystery.

1869
Louis Riel leads his Métis followers in the Red River Rebellion.

1871
British Columbia joins Canada.

1755
The British expel the entire French population of Acadia (today's Maritime provinces), sending them into exile.

1776
The 13 Colonies revolt against Britain, and the Loyalists flee to Canada.

1837
Calling for responsible government, the Patriotes, following Louis-Joseph Papineau, rebel in Lower Canada; William Lyon Mackenzie leads the uprising in Upper Canada.

1867
New Brunswick, Nova Scotia and the United Province of Canada come together in Confederation to form the Dominion of Canada.

1870
Manitoba joins Canada. The Northwest Territories become an official territory of Canada.

1784
Rachel

Timeline

1885
At Craigellachie, British Columbia, the last spike is driven to complete the building of the Canadian Pacific Railway.

1898
The Yukon Territory becomes an official territory of Canada.

1914
Britain declares war on Germany, and Canada, because of its ties to Britain, is at war too.

1918
As a result of the Wartime Elections Act, the women of Canada are given the right to vote in federal elections.

1945
World War II ends conclusively with the dropping of atomic bombs on Hiroshima and Nagasaki.

1873
Prince Edward Island joins Canada.

1896
Gold is discovered on Bonanza Creek, a tributary of the Klondike River.

1905
Alberta and Saskatchewan join Canada.

1917
In the Halifax harbour, two ships collide, causing an explosion that leaves more than 1,600 dead and 9,000 injured.

1939
Canada declares war on Germany seven days after war is declared by Britain and France.

1949
Newfoundland, under the leadership of Joey Smallwood, joins Canada.

1901
Keeley

1885
Marie-Claire

1914
Millie

Dear Reader,

Did you enjoy reading this Our Canadian Girl adventure? Write us and tell us what you think! We'd love to hear about your favourite parts, which characters you like best, and even whom else you'd like to see stories about. Maybe you'd like to read an adventure with one of Our Canadian Girls that happened in your hometown—fifty, a hundred years ago or more!

Send your letters to:

Our Canadian Girl
c/o Penguin Canada
10 Alcorn Avenue, Suite 300
Toronto, ON M4V 3B2

Be sure to check your bookstore for more books in the Our Canadian Girl series. There are some ready for you right now, and more are on their way.

We look forward to hearing from you!

Sincerely,
Barbara Berson
PENGUIN GROUP (CANADA)

P.S. Don't forget to visit us online at www.ourcanadiangirl.ca—there are some other girls you should meet!